THE JACKAL AN[...]

ONE DAY, WHILE ROAMING IN THE FOREST IN SEARCH OF FOOD, A JACKAL SUDDENLY SPIED A TROOP OF RATS. THEIR KING WAS A HUGE BANDICOOT.

I COULD ATTACK THEM. BUT THEN I'D CATCH ONLY ONE AND THE REST WOULD RUN AWAY.

IF I'M CLEVER, HOWEVER, THESE RATS COULD PROVIDE ME WITH FOOD FOR MANY DAYS.

SO HE FOLLOWED THEM TO THEIR HOLE.

WHEN THE LAST OF THEM HAD GONE INTO THE HOLE, THE JACKAL STOOD OUTSIDE ON ONE LEG, HIS MOUTH OPEN AND HIS FACE TURNED TOWARDS THE SUN.

A LITTLE LATER, WHEN THE RATS CAME OUT AGAIN—

WHY ARE YOU STANDING ON ONE LEG?

IF I STOOD ON ALL FOUR, THE EARTH WOULD NOT BE ABLE TO BEAR MY WEIGHT.

WHY DO YOU KEEP YOUR MOUTH OPEN?

TO TAKE IN AIR, MY ONLY FOOD.

AND WHY IS YOUR FACE TURNED UPWARDS?

TO WORSHIP THE SUN.

HOW LUCKY WE ARE TO HAVE A SAINT IN OUR MIDST! WE SHALL WORSHIP HIM EVERY MORNING AND EVENING.

IT HAS WORKED! HE REALLY THINKS I AM A SAINT!

THE NEXT MORNING—

AH! HERE THEY COME. I MUST POSE AGAIN FOR THEM.

SO THAT EVENING AS THE RATS WERE READY TO SET OUT—

TODAY ALL OF YOU GO AHEAD. I'LL COME OUT LAST.

IF MY GUESS IS CORRECT, HE'LL POUNCE ON ME. I MUST BE READY.

THE NEXT MOMENT THE JACKAL SPRANG AT HIM...

...BUT MISSED.

SO THIS IS YOUR GAME! YOU RASCAL!

THE BANDICOOT DUG HIS TEETH INTO THE JACKAL'S THROAT AND KILLED HIM.

BACK CAME ALL THE OTHER RATS AND THEY HAD A GRAND FEAST.

THE JACKAL AND THE LION

GR. GR

A HUNGRY JACKAL ONCE SUDDENLY CAME ACROSS A LION WHO WAS ON HIS WAY HOME.

WHAT DO YOU WANT?

I CANNOT HOPE TO ESCAPE. IT WOULD BE WISER TO PLAY HUMBLE.

MY LORD, PLEASE LET ME BE YOUR HUMBLE SERVANT.

ALL RIGHT.

WHAT LUCK! I'LL NEVER HAVE TO GO HUNGRY AGAIN.

FOLLOW ME.

WHEN THEY REACHED THE LION'S DEN—

IF YOU DO AS I TELL YOU, YOU WILL BE WELL FED.

YOUR WORD IS MY COMMAND, MY LORD.

YOU WILL GO TO THE TOP OF THE MOUNTAIN EACH DAY AND SEE IF THERE ARE ANY ANIMALS ROAMING IN THE VALLEY BELOW.

AND IF I SEE ONE, MY LORD?

YOU WILL COME AND TELL ME ABOUT IT. THEN YOU WILL SAY: "SHINE FORTH IN ALL YOUR MIGHT, MY LORD."

THEN, AFTER I'VE KILLED THE ANIMAL AND EATEN MY FILL, YOU MAY TAKE WHAT'S LEFT.

SO THE NEXT DAY THE JACKAL WENT TO THE MOUNTAIN TOP.

HE SPED BACK TO THE LION...

...AND FELL AT HIS FEET.

THE LION KILLED THE ELEPHANT...

...AND ATE HIS FILL.

NOW YOU MAY EAT THE REST.

AS THE DAYS WENT BY, THE JACKAL GREW FATTER AND FATTER.

BUT, ALAS! HE GREW LESS AND LESS HUMBLE. ONE DAY—

WHY SHOULD I LIVE ON LEFTOVER FOOD? I, TOO, AM A FOUR-FOOTED CREATURE! WHY WORK FOR THE LION WHEN I COULD KILL ELEPHANTS AND BUFFALOES FOR MYSELF?

AFTER ALL, THE LION ONLY GETS HIS STRENGTH FROM THE MAGIC PHRASE, "GO FORTH AND SHINE IN ALL YOUR MIGHT".

HE APPEALED TO THE LION.

MY LORD, I HAVE LIVED FOR TOO LONG ON WHAT YOU KILL. I WOULD LIKE TO EAT AN ELEPHANT I HAVE KILLED MYSELF.

THE LION WAS SILENT FOR A WHILE.

WHAT A FOOLISH IDEA! HE'LL BE KILLED HIMSELF!

O JACKAL, ONLY LIONS CAN KILL ELEPHANTS. GIVE UP THIS SILLY IDEA. AND BE HAPPY TO EAT WHAT I KILL.

PLEASE, MY LORD. DON'T DENY ME THIS CHANCE. I'LL WAIT HERE, WHILE YOU GO TO THE MOUNTAIN-TOP.

WHEN YOU SEE AN ELEPHANT, COME TO ME AND SAY, "SHINE FORTH IN ALL YOUR MIGHT, JACKAL," AND I'M SURE TO KILL IT.

AT LAST THE LION GAVE IN.

ALL RIGHT. I'LL DO IT.

A LITTLE LATER, THE LION CAME BACK.

I HAVE JUST SPIED AN ELEPHANT COMING THIS WAY. SHINE FORTH IN ALL YOUR MIGHT, JACKAL.

THE JACKAL NIMBLY BOUNDED AWAY...

...ON THE TRAIL OF THE ELEPHANT.

I'LL CATCH HIM BY THE THROAT AND KILL HIM.

HE SPRANG AT THE ELEPHANT...

...BUT MISSED HIM.

THE PUZZLED ELEPHANT JUST WALKED OVER HIM...

...AND THAT WAS THE END OF THE FOOLHARDY JACKAL.

THE CLEVER JACKAL

A GROUP OF ROGUES WERE ONCE HAVING A GRAND PARTY.

TOWARDS MIDNIGHT—

CAN I HAVE SOME MORE MEAT?

YOU CAN HAVE MORE WINE IF YOU LIKE, BUT THERE'S NO MEAT LEFT.

WHAT! NO MEAT! BUT I MUST HAVE SOME!

I'LL GO TO THE CHARNEL-GROVE, KILL A PROWLING JACKAL, AND BRING YOU ITS MEAT.

CLUB IN HAND, THE BRAGGART SWAGGERED OFF.

WHEN HE REACHED THE GROVE —

I'LL PRETEND I'M A CORPSE. THAT WILL ATTRACT JACKALS AND KEEP AWAY LIONS AND TIGERS.

WHEN A JACKAL COMES NEAR, I'LL KILL HIM WITH MY CLUB.

A LITTLE LATER, A PACK OF JACKALS CAME BY.

LOOK, THERE'S A CORPSE. COME ON!

WAIT! LET ME MAKE SURE WE'RE SAFE.

SNIFF! SNIFF!

THE SMELL OF A LIVING MAN! JUST AS I THOUGHT! HE IS ONLY PRETENDING TO BE DEAD.

JUST THEN HE NOTICED THE CLUB.

HE IS PROBABLY WAITING TO KILL ONE OF US.

WAIT HERE. I'LL TAKE CARE OF THE RASCAL.

HE CREPT UP TO THE MAN! · · ·

· · · CAUGHT THE CLUB WITH HIS TEETH · · ·

· · · AND GAVE IT A SLIGHT TUG.

IT MUST BE A BANDICOOT! I'D BETTER TIGHTEN MY GRIP.

THE NEXT MOMENT THE JACKAL LET GO OF THE CLUB WITH A JERK.

THE STARTLED ROGUE JUMPED TO HIS FEET, FLUNG HIS CLUB AT THE JACKAL...

... AND MISSED!

I DARE NOT FACE MY FRIENDS AFTER MY VAIN BOAST.

I'D BETTER GO HOME AND SLEEP.

THE JACKAL AND THE MAGIC SPELL

IN A SECLUDED SPOT IN A FOREST, THE FAMILY PRIEST OF BRAHMADATTA, KING OF VARANASI, WAS ONCE REPEATING A SECRET SPELL.

A JACKAL LYING NEAR BY PRICKED UP HIS EARS.

IF I LISTEN CAREFULLY I, TOO, CAN MASTER THAT.

A LITTLE LATER THE BRAHMAN GOT UP.

THERE! I'VE MASTERED IT.

THE NEXT MOMENT, TO HIS SURPRISE, A JACKAL STOOD BEFORE HIM.

HO! BRAHMAN, YOU COULDN'T HAVE MASTERED THE SPELL BETTER THAN I.

AND OFF HE RAN. THE PRIEST RAN AFTER HIM.

I MUST CATCH HIM! HE'LL PLAY HAVOC WITH THAT SPELL.

BUT THE JACKAL ESCAPED DEEP INTO THE FOREST.

I'LL FIRST GET MARRIED AND THEN, USING THE SPELL, I'LL BRING ALL THE FOUR-FOOTED CREATURES OF THE FOREST UNDER MY SWAY.

HE SOON FOUND HIMSELF A SHE-JACKAL.

IF YOU BECOME MY WIFE YOU SHALL BE QUEEN OF ALL THE ANIMALS OF THE FOREST.

I'M WILLING.

SNIFF SNIFF

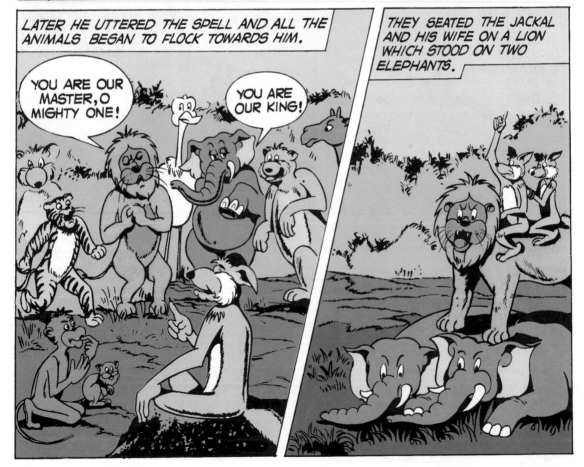

LATER HE UTTERED THE SPELL AND ALL THE ANIMALS BEGAN TO FLOCK TOWARDS HIM.

YOU ARE OUR MASTER, O MIGHTY ONE!

YOU ARE OUR KING!

THEY SEATED THE JACKAL AND HIS WIFE ON A LION WHICH STOOD ON TWO ELEPHANTS.

THEY CONFERRED A TITLE ON THE JACKAL AND BOWED TO HIM.

HAIL SARVADATA, CHOSEN KING OF THE ANIMALS!

HAIL!

HAIL!

ALL THIS WENT TO THE JACKAL'S HEAD.

MY SUBJECTS, WE SHALL CAPTURE THE CITY OF VARANASI.

SO, WITH HIS GREAT FOLLOWING, HE MARCHED TO VARANASI.

WE SHALL CAMP HERE AND SEND A MESSAGE TO THE KING.

WHEN THE KING RECEIVED THE MESSAGE, HIS FAMILY PRIEST WAS WITH HIM.

"SURRENDER YOUR KINGDOM OR DIE FIGHTING FOR IT," HE SAYS.

HE HAS STRUCK TERROR EVERYWHERE. HIS CAMP COVERS AN AREA OF THIRTY-SIX MILES! WHO IS THIS ANIMAL?

HE IS SARVADATA, THE JACKAL-KING. LEAVE HIM TO ME. I'LL FIND A WAY OF DEFEATING HIM.

ALL RIGHT. MAY YOU BE SUCCESSFUL.

I MUST FIRST FIND OUT WHAT HE INTENDS TO DO.

O SARVADATA, HOW DO YOU PLAN TO TAKE THIS CITY?

I WILL MAKE THE LIONS ROAR AND CREATE PANIC AND CHAOS AMONG THE PEOPLE. THEN I WILL MARCH INTO THE CITY.

OH! SO THAT'S IT!

19

SEEING THE ELEPHANTS RUN AMUCK, ALL THE ANIMALS BROKE INTO A STAMPEDE AND RAN HELTER SKELTER.

IN THE STAMPEDE, THE JACKALS WERE TRAMPLED TO DEATH.

THAT WAS THE END OF KING SARVADATA WHO HAD DARED TO DREAM OF CONQUERING VARANASI.

THE JACKAL AND THE OTTERS

A JACKAL'S WIFE ONCE WANTED TO EAT SOME FRESH ROHITA FISH. PROMISING TO BRING IT FOR HER, THE JACKAL WENT TO THE RIVER.

JUST THEN HE SAW TWO OTTERS DRAGGING ALONG A HUGE ROHITA FISH.

WHAT'S THE MATTER, FRIENDS?

THIS FISH WAS CAUGHT BY BOTH OF US. WE CANNOT DECIDE HOW TO DIVIDE IT.

WILL YOU DO IT FOR US?

JUST AS I EXPECTED!

CERTAINLY! YOU CAN LEAVE IT TO ME. I'VE SETTLED MANY CASES BEFORE AND SETTLED THEM FAIRLY.

THE JACKAL THEN CUT OFF THE HEAD AND THE TAIL OF THE FISH.

YOU TAKE THE HEAD...

THE JACKAL AND THE SHE-GOAT

LONG AGO, IN A CAVE ON THE SLOPES OF THE HIMALAYAS, THERE LIVED A HERD OF WILD GOATS. ONE DAY, AS A JACKAL AND HIS MATE WERE PROWLING ABOUT FOR FOOD, THEY SAW THE GOATS GRAZING.

COME! LET US KILL ONE OF THEM.

WAIT! IF WE ARE CLEVER, WE'LL HAVE FOOD ENOUGH FOR MANY MONTHS.

THEY WAITED TILL THE GOATS BEGAN TO WANDER APART AS THEY GRAZED.

LET'S FOLLOW THAT ONE TILL HE IS FAR AWAY FROM THE OTHERS.

A FEW HOURS LATER —

THERE! I'VE KILLED HIM. NOW HELP ME DRAG HIM TO OUR CAVE.

MANY MONTHS PASSED AND, ONE BY ONE, THE GOATS WERE EATEN BY THE JACKALS.

THE ONLY ONE LEFT WAS A WISE SHE-GOAT.

I DARE NOT GO OUT. THE JACKALS ARE ABOUT AGAIN!

THAT SHE-GOAT SEEMS TO BE WISE TO US. SHE DOES NOT COME OUT AT ALL.

THE JACKAL HAD AN IDEA.

YOU GO ALONE EVERY DAY AND TRY TO WIN HER CONFIDENCE. WHEN SHE BEGINS TO TRUST YOU I WILL LIE OUTSIDE OUR CAVE AND PRETEND TO BE DEAD. AND YOU··· BZZ. BZZ····

EAGER TO CARRY OUT THE PLAN, THE SHE-JACKAL HASTENED TO THE GOAT'S CAVE.

O WISE GOAT, DO YOU LIVE HERE ALL ALONE?

IT'S THE WIFE OF THE JACKAL!

PLEASE DON'T BE AFRAID. I'VE COME TO MAKE FRIENDS WITH YOU. PLEASE COME OUT.

NO! I DON'T TRUST YOU. GO AWAY. YOU KILLED ALL MY RELATIVES.

IT WAS MY HUSBAND, NOT ME. IF YOU DON'T TRUST ME, YOU NEEDN'T COME OUT. BUT, PLEASE, DON'T REFUSE TO TALK TO ME.

THERE'S NO HARM IN SPEAKING TO HER FROM INSIDE. SHE MAY BE INNOCENT.

I AM VERY UNHAPPY. NO ONE IS WILLING TO BE MY FRIEND, BECAUSE OF MY HUSBAND'S EVIL WAYS.

THE KIND-HEARTED GOAT FELT SORRY FOR THE SHE-JACKAL.

PLEASE DON'T SAY THAT. I'LL BE YOUR FRIEND.

AS EACH DAY PASSED THE SHE-GOAT'S TRUST IN THE JACKAL INCREASED, TILL ONE DAY—

TOMORROW WE SHALL CARRY OUT THE NEXT PART OF OUR PLAN.

THE NEXT DAY—

OH, I AM LEFT ALL ALONE! MY HUSBAND IS DEAD. PLEASE COME AND HELP ME BURY HIM.

NO! NO! I CANNOT COME. I'M AFRAID OF HIM.

BUT WHAT HARM CAN HE DO TO YOU NOW THAT HE IS DEAD?

DEAD OR ALIVE, HE'S CRUEL AND I'M AFRAID TO COME OUT.

AND I HAD THOUGHT YOU WERE MY FRIEND! HOW UNFORTUNATE I AM THAT I MUST BURY MY HUSBAND ALL BY MYSELF!

SHE CAN'T BE LYING. HE MUST REALLY BE DEAD.

DON'T WEEP, MY FRIEND. I'LL COME WITH YOU.

AS THEY WERE ABOUT TO SET OUT, HOWEVER, THE SHE-GOAT SUDDENLY BECAME DOUBTFUL AGAIN.

FRIEND, YOU WALK AHEAD AND SHOW ME THE WAY. I'LL FOLLOW.

A LITTLE LATER—

AH, FOOTSTEPS! HERE THEY COME.

HE FORGOT THAT HE WAS SUPPOSED TO PLAY DEAD, AND OPENED HIS EYES TO LOOK AT THE PLUMP GOAT.

HE'S ALIVE!

THE WICKED WRETCH WANTS TO KILL ME. THEY ARE BOTH TRAITORS!

WHEN SHE HAD GONE —

HUMPH! I THOUGHT YOU HAD WON HER CONFIDENCE!

I HAD! BUT YOU, MY LORD, HAD TO BE A FOOL AND SPOIL IT ALL.

THE JACKAL WAS SO CRESTFALLEN THAT HIS MATE FELT SORRY FOR HIM.

DON'T LOOK SO UNHAPPY! I'LL BRING HER AGAIN. THIS TIME, BE ON YOUR GUARD.

AH! MY FRIEND, YOU HAVE PERFORMED A MIRACLE! AS YOU CAME NEAR HIM, MY HUSBAND CAME TO LIFE AGAIN. HE WANTS TO MEET YOU AND THANK YOU.

THE TRAITOR! SHE TAKES ME TO BE A TRUSTING FOOL. I'LL TEACH HER A LESSON SHE'LL NEVER FORGET!

THE SHE-GOAT CAME OUT.

ALL RIGHT, I'LL COME — WITH AN ESCORT OF TWO THOUSAND DOGS. IF THEY DO NOT FIND ENOUGH FOOD, THEY WILL DEVOUR YOU AND YOUR MATE. SO HURRY HOME AND PREPARE ENOUGH FOOD FOR US ALL!

THE RUSE WORKED.

TWO THOUSAND DOGS! I'VE HAD ENOUGH OF THIS GOAT.

DEAR FRIEND, I'VE CHANGED MY MIND. YOU'D BETTER NOT COME. YOUR CAVE MIGHT BE BURGLED WHILE YOU ARE AWAY.

BUT I WANT TO COME AND....

NO! PLEASE DON'T BOTHER. SOME OTHER TIME, PERHAPS.

THEN SHE RAN FOR HER LIFE...

...TILL SHE REACHED HER MATE.

QUICK! WE MUST RUN. OR ELSE WE'LL MAKE A MEAL FOR TWO THOUSAND DOGS!

TWO THOUSAND DOGS!

THE JACKAL AND HIS MATE TOOK TO THEIR HEELS. AND THEY WERE NOT SEEN OR HEARD OF EVER AGAIN.

THE ACK QUIZ
FOLKTALES AND FABLES

1 Who is the author of the Panchatantra?

2 Which stories tell of the previous births of Buddha?

3 Identify the person standing beside Buddha in the picture.

4 What was this person's garland made of?

5 What was Gautama Buddha's name when he was a prince?

6 Who is the king in the picture?

7 Who is the minister in the picture?

8 What is the original name of the minister?

9 Who was the famous wit in Krishnadevaraya's court?

10 How many books is the Hitopadesha divided into?